THOMAS & FRIENDS

THE GREAT RACE

THE MOVIE

Illustrated by Tommy Stubbs

 A GOLDEN BOOK · NEW YORK

Thomas the Tank Engine & Friends™

CREATED BY BRITT ALLCROFT

Based on the Railway Series by the Reverend W Awdry.
© 2016 Gullane (Thomas) LLC. Thomas the Tank Engine & Friends and Thomas & Friends are trademarks of Gullane (Thomas) Limited.
Thomas the Tank Engine & Friends and Design Is Reg. U.S. Pat. & Tm. Off. © 2016 HIT Entertainment Limited. All rights reserved.
Published in the United States by Golden Books, an imprint of Random House Chi̇̇ldren's Books, a division of Penguin Random House
LLC, 1745 Broadway, New York, NY 10019, and in Canada by Penguin Random Hȯ̇use [...] ̇̇rs, A Golden
Book, A Big Golden Book, the G colophon, and the distinctive gold spine are regi̇̇ [...] se LLC.
ISBN 978-1-101-93798-3 (trade) — ISBN 978-1-1 [...]
randomhousekids.com   www.thomasaṅ̇ [...]
Printed in the United States of Aṙ̇ [...]
10 9 8 7 6 5 4 3 2 1
Random House Children's Books supports the First Amendmė̇ [...]

D1511866

HiT entertainment

One sunny day on the Island of Sodor, Thomas the Tank Engine chuffed into Vicarstown Station and saw a shiny new engine. Gordon pulled up next to Thomas and sighed. "That's my brother. They call him the Flying Scotsman."

The new engine said he was going to the Great Railway Show on the Mainland. "That's where engines compete to see who's the fastest and the strongest. But I'm not sure any engines from Sodor will be going."

Thomas' rods rattled with excitement. He really wanted to go.

Thomas found Sir Topham Hatt and suggested that some streamlining be added to an engine from Sodor so it could win races at the show.

"That is an excellent idea," Sir Topham Hatt said. "Once he's been streamlined, Gordon will be faster than ever."

Gordon! That was *not* what Thomas had in mind!

The next day, a railway ferry made a very exciting delivery to Brendam Docks. Thomas watched as engines from all over the world rolled ashore.

"Where are you going?" the Dock Manager asked.

"The Great Railway Show," puffed a streamlined Belgian engine.

"That's happening on the Mainland," the Manager replied.

The engines jostled and pushed past Thomas as they returned to the ferry.

A brightly painted engine named Ashima rushed for the departing ferry—and bumped into Thomas!

"Whoa!" he peeped as he teetered on the edge of the quay.

Dockworkers quickly wrapped a chain around Thomas' coupling hook. With Ashima's help, they pulled him back from the edge.

Ashima apologized for bumping Thomas and asked if there was another way to the Mainland since she'd now missed her ferry.

But Thomas didn't answer. He just chugged away in a huff.

"I don't see why *she* should get to go to the Great Railway Show," Thomas puffed to his carriages.

"Well, she's very beautifully painted," Clarabel suggested.

"Any engine can get painted," Thomas puffed.

Suddenly Thomas had another idea. He unhooked his carriages and sped to the Steamworks.

Thomas told Victor he needed to be repainted. "I was thinking maybe lightning bolts and racing stripes."

But just as Victor went to work, Sir Topham Hatt stopped by to check on Gordon's streamlining. He liked the idea of a speedy-looking paint job—but not for Thomas.

Meanwhile, over at the Dieselworks, Diesel had an idea of his own. He wanted to disguise Paxton, Den, and Dart as his trucks and pretend to pull them.

"I'll look like I'm pulling a very heavy train all by myself," he announced with a snicker. "And if Sir Topham Hatt thinks I'm stronger than Henry, he'll take *me* to the Great Railway Show instead."

Later that day, Thomas met Ashima again. She didn't understand why Thomas had wanted to be painted like her. "You can only be you," she tooted. "Every engine I've ever known was useful and had a job they could do." Ashima asked Thomas if he was good at shunting and sorting trucks.

"Yes," Thomas peeped. And then he had his best idea yet for going to the Great Railway Show. "I'll show Sir Topham Hatt what *I* can do best!"

The next morning Thomas went to Knapford Station to practice his shunting, but the rails were blocked by Diesel's tricky trucks. Thomas decided to move them himself.

"What are you doing?" Diesel hissed. "You'll spoil my trick!"

The disguised diesels started to chug along with Thomas. He was surprised by how easily everything moved—and how quickly!

There was a red signal ahead. Thomas tried to stop, but the diesels kept pushing because they couldn't hear the warning bell.

CRASH! Thomas collided with a passing engine named Norman.

It was the day of the Great Railway Show, and all the engines Sir Topham Hatt had chosen were ready to go. Gordon had been painted and streamlined. He even had a new nameplate: The Shooting Star.

Sir Topham Hatt had wanted Thomas to go for the Shunting Challenge, but now Thomas needed to be repaired after his accident. Percy would go in his place.

Thomas tooted goodbye to the engines. He even wished Ashima good luck.

Later that morning, Victor and Kevin discovered that Gordon's safety valve had never been installed after his streamlining! Without the valve, Gordon could dangerously overheat during his race.

Even though his own repairs weren't finished, Thomas took the valve and steamed across Vicarstown Bridge to the Mainland.

Thomas reached the Great Railway Show. He eagerly searched the crowds of visiting engines and found Gordon on the starting line of the Great Race.

But Gordon wouldn't listen to Thomas. "Nonsense! The team at the Steamworks is very efficient. And besides, the race is starting *now*!"

A whistle blew, green flags waved, and the engines took off!

Gordon raced along the tracks, passing engines. "Shooting Star coming through!" he announced loudly.

But suddenly his face turned red and steam hissed from inside his streamlining.

Gordon's brother, the Flying Scotsman, tried to warn him that something was wrong, but Gordon wouldn't listen . . . until his boiler burst! He sputtered to a stop in a cloud of steam as the other engines sped on.

"Oh, the indignity," he peeped.

Meanwhile, over at the Shunting Challenge, Percy was too scared to enter the race. He wanted Thomas to compete in his place.

"Okay," Thomas peeped. "But I might lose, you know."

But Thomas didn't lose. He chuffed through round after round, pulling tankers and flatbeds into line. He beat big engines from Russia, Italy, and Brazil.

In the end, there were only two engines left—Thomas and Ashima!

A whistle blew, and the final challenge began.

The two engines steamed back and forth, buffering boxcars into place. Soon their sidings were full, and it was a race to the finish line. But then Thomas noticed an overturned truck on Ashima's track! He sped along to push it out of her way.

Ashima raced to victory.

"Thomas, you let me win," Ashima peeped.

"I know," Thomas replied. "But it wouldn't have been fair. Your track was blocked."

Soon after, everyone gathered for the award ceremony. "We would like to declare *two* winners in the Shunting Challenge," announced a judge. Ashima had won for the fastest time, and Thomas had also won—for helping his competitor.

All the engines whistled and cheered. Even Gordon's brother, the Flying Scotsman, admitted that he was impressed with the engines from Sodor.

The Great Railway Show   START and FINISH   The Great Railway Show